"Warm Fuzzies"

What Happened the Moment I Knew About You

L.A. Bogedin

Balboa Press books may be ordered through booksellers or by contacting:

Balboa Press
A Division of Hay House
1663 Liberty Drive
Bloomington, IN 47403
www.balboapress.com
1 (877) 407-4847

Because of the dynamic nature of the Internet, any web addresses or links contained in this book may have changed since publication and may no longer be valid. The views expressed in this work are solely those of the author and do not necessarily reflect the views of the publisher, and the publisher hereby disclaims any responsibility for them.

Any people depicted in stock imagery provided by Thinkstock are models, and such images are being used for illustrative purposes only.
Certain stock imagery © Thinkstock.

ISBN: 978-1-4525-9951-9 (sc)
ISBN: 978-1-4525-9952-6 (e)

Library of Congress Control Number: 2014921168

Print information available on the last page.

Balboa Press rev. date: 2/27/2015

BALBOA.
PRESS
A DIVISION OF HAY HOUSE

I present this book to
Avery Bogedin and all my grandkids to come.

Thank you,
Karen Antosh, Ingrid Carson, Brittney
Lopes, Hildy Morgan, and
Ryan and Jenn Bogedin.

Go jump in your jammies and snuggle in tight,
For this is the story of what happened one night.

A silly old goose let her heart fill with love,
And the news of you coming gave it a shove.

Just like bathwater bubbles go pop, pop and pop,
My hardly used heart didn't know when to stop.

Once the love started flowing, it grew and it grew.
I can tell you right now there was but one thing to do!

SO...

I whirled and I twirled and I danced all around.
Then I started to sing and jump up and down.

What I have to say now is a bit hard to swallow.
I was a grumpy old goose and
let my heart become hollow.

I found this out fast and I know you'll agree
If you don't use your heart, it empties quickly.

But I couldn't stop grinning, and I couldn't stop spinning.
I knew for a fact this was just the beginning!

The thought of us meeting brought tears of delight,
And my heart just got bigger—it was really a sight.

Not having been used and now filled to the max,
I started to notice what I thought were some cracks.

Like a silly old goose, I had rattled it loose.
While my ticker was filling, the cracks started spilling.

Then my heart did something I'd rather have skipped.
My hardly used heart started to drip!

Like an overfilled bathtub that no one had drained,
Love ran down the sides under all of the strain.

My heart was so full, it could not be contained.
It leaked out all over. How could I explain?

My daft heart went bonkers, and my love it did spill.
It gathered in puddles and a lake it soon filled.

It wobbled, and teetered, and clanged with a crash.
It burst into pieces with a belly flop splash!

It burst right apart like yummy corn popping,
But I couldn't stop hopping to do any mopping.

My heart needed fixing—that much I could see,
Gosh, there were so many pieces and only one me.

I knew that for you, I just had to try.
But where should I start? I thought with a sigh.

Finding a patch was the first thing to do,
But where on this earth would I find that much glue?

11

So I picked up the pieces right where they had landed
And squished them together for lack of a bandage.

As if you had every detail well planned,
You stepped right in and gave me a hand.

A warm, fuzzy feeling started to grow.
It stretched from my head to the tips of my toes.

Before the "warm fuzzies," I'll tell you quite frankly,
My empty old heart had made me quite cranky!

What warm fuzzies were, I hadn't a clue,
But I started to think the warm fuzzies were you.

Like a big sponge, the warm fuzzies expanded
And soaked up the love, fixing my heart single-handed.

My soggy old ticker that once had gone pop,
Was now filled with love and held every drop.

The warm fuzzies grew and you wrapped up my heart,
It goes without saying, you're brilliantly smart!

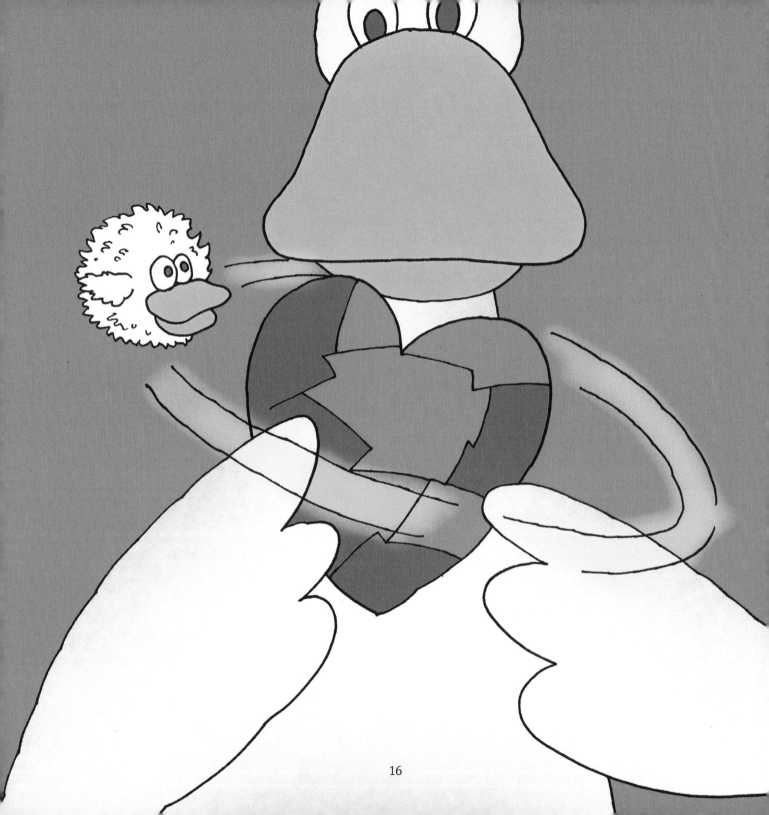

You sealed up my heart with your warm, fuzzy fluff.
I'll tell you right now that I'm filled with the stuff.

Fuzz-stuffing my heart was really quite sneaky.
With you in the world, my heart will never be leaky.

My fuzzy-filled heart might be lumpy and bumpy,
But now it just giggles and never is grumpy.

I know it sounds silly, but, believe me, it's true—
My fuzzy-filled heart feels just like brand-new!

So this is the story of the way that it was.
All this happened in seconds. Love usually does.

I want you to know that my heart you did mend.
I am hoping someday to be your best friend.

When we are friends, I know sure enough,
I'll still have some extra, of that warm fuzzy fluff.

And someday, just maybe, you'll let me do
Some warm, fuzzy filling of your sweet heart too.

Now this silly old goose has a heart full of fuzz,
But that's not why I love you...

I love you just because!

CPSIA information can be obtained
at www.ICGtesting.com
Printed in the USA
LVOW05s1930220216
476256LV00016B/65/P